Agatha Parrot

AND THE Heart of Mud

TYPED OUT NEATLY BY
KJARTAN POSKITT

ILLUSTRATED BY
WES HARGIS

HOUGHTON MIFFLIN HARCOURT

BOSTON   NEW YORK

The Library of Congress has cataloged the hardcover as follows:
Poskitt, Kjartan, author. | Hargis, Wes, illustrator.
Title: Agatha Parrot and the heart of mud / neatly typed out by Kjartan
Poskitt ; art by Wes Hargis.
Description: First US edition. | Boston ; New York : Clarion Books, Houghton
Mifflin Harcourt, 2016. | "Originally published in the United Kingdom by
Egmont UK Ltd." | Summary: When Agatha Parrot joins the spelling club to
support her new friend Martha, she gets help from an unexpected
source—her cousin, Bella, who thinks she is emailing Agatha's brother.
Identifiers: LCCN 2015041138
Subjects: | CYAC: English language—Spelling—Fiction. | Family life—Fiction. |
Email—Fiction. | Humorous stories. | BISAC: JUVENILE FICTION / Humorous Stories.
| JUVENILE FICTION / Sports & Recreation / Soccer. | JUVENILE FICTION / School
& Education. | JUVENILE FICTION / Love & Romance. | JUVENILE FICTION /
Holidays & Celebrations / Valentine's Day. | JUVENILE FICTION / Girls & Women.
Classification: LCC PZ7.1.P65 Ad 2016 | DDC [Fic]—dc23
LC record available at https://lccn.loc.gov/2015041138

ISBN: 978-0-544-50876-7 hardcover
ISBN: 978-1-328-74212-4 paperback

Manufactured in the United States of America
DOC 10 9 8 7 6 5 4 3 2 1

4500681376

This book is dedicated to
Auntie Zoe,
Who is so nice, so cool,
so stylish,
and SO like me.

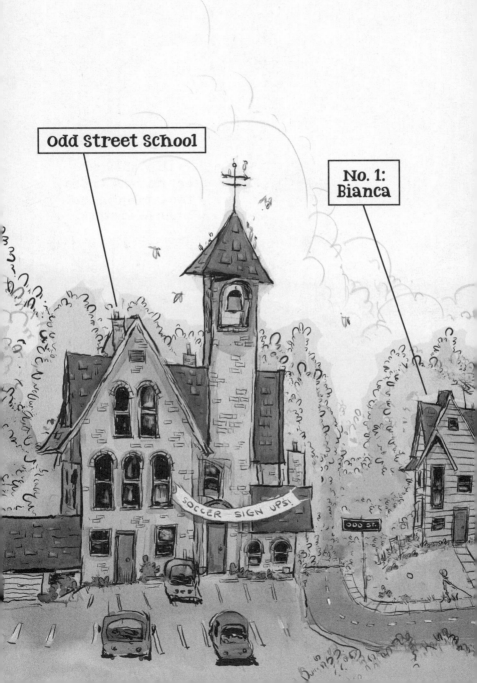

Contents

The Heart of . . . What? 1

The Return of the Mud Creature 4

The Best of Enemies 19

Nice and Friendly and Boring 26

Welcome to the Club 33

What??? 47

Zogs and Debras 49

Inside Information 62

Ivy Malting and Her
Secret-Message-Sending Leg 65

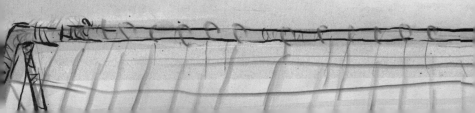

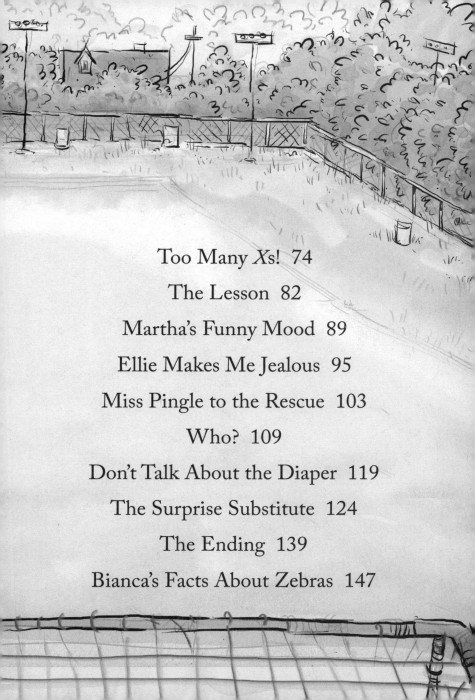

Too Many *X*s! 74

The Lesson 82

Martha's Funny Mood 89

Ellie Makes Me Jealous 95

Miss Pingle to the Rescue 103

Who? 109

Don't Talk About the Diaper 119

The Surprise Substitute 124

The Ending 139

Bianca's Facts About Zebras 147

The Heart of ...
What?

Hiya! I'm Agatha Jane Parrot and THANKS for reading this book. It's very nice of you, because the title is a bit strange!

If you want to know why this book is called *The Heart of Mud*, it's something that somebody says later on in the story. If you like, you can flip through the pages and see if you can spot who says it. Remember, you're on page 2 now, so I'll wait here and you can come back when you've found it.

I'll just hum some waiting music . . . *Tum-tee-tiddly-tum!*

If you think the title is kind of silly, it could have been a LOT worse. There's one part in the story where my friend Ivy sends secret messages with her leg! It's true. She really does, so Ivy wanted this book to be called *Ivy Malting and Her Secret-Message-Sending Leg.* Ha ha! But it was too long to fit on the front, so we used that title for one of the chapters instead.

Before we start, I should warn you that this book does have a bit of LOVE in it. (That's why it has *Heart* in the title.)

Don't worry. There's no long kissing or holding

hands or anything
gross like that.
YUCK! We
don't do that
sort of thing on
Odd Street—
except once. It was
Dad's birthday, so Mom had
to give him a kiss, but they

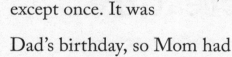

didn't like it much because he's bald and she's got
hairy legs. What a pity Mom couldn't take the
hairs off her legs and plant them on Dad's head!
That would have been an **awesome** birthday
present for him. How very thoughtful.

Anyway, Ivy's leg is waiting for you, so we'd better get on with the story. WAHOO!

The Return of the Mud Creature

In our house, Wednesday's dinner is the BEST dinner of the week.

What makes Wednesday so good is that Mom cooks up "A Real Taste of Italy." It's made with fresh pasta and handpicked tomatoes with an exciting blend of herbs and covered with a rich cheese sauce. Each serving also contains 377 calories, 13 grams of fat, and 832 mg of sodium (whatever that means).

How do I know all this? Because that's what it says on the box. YUM!

We love dinner from a box. Even Dad can't cook it wrong, except for the time he forgot to poke holes in the top with a fork and it went *BADDOOF* in the microwave. The smell lasted for weeks! Mom went ballistic, but secretly she was happy, because when her friends came over they thought she'd been cooking fancy stuff like they do on TV.

"What IS that lovely smell?" said the friends.

"It's my new secret recipe," said Mom, the Big Fibber.

Gosh, if I told whoppers like that, I'd be sent straight to bed with no arguing.

The bad thing is that we can only have box dinner on Wednesdays, because Wednesday is the only day when there are four of us for dinner. The box says *serves four* and WE MUST OBEY the box.

So anyway, one Wednesday we were all sitting around the table waiting for our exciting herbs and 13 grams of fat. The four of us were Mom, Dad, me, and my little sister, Tilly. As usual, Tilly was dressed as a fairy, and she was watching the numbers on the microwave count down so she could do her magic spell at the end.

"Five, four, three, two, one . . ." said the fairy. Then she waved her wand.

PING! went the microwave oven.

Dad got the plastic box thing out and peeled the top back. *Oh wow, smell that smell, love it love it*. He was just dolloping it out onto four plates when we heard an evil scraping sound coming from outside.

The front gate squeaked and the scraping sound got closer, and then the front door burst open. A hideous creature covered in mud staggered into the hallway, leaving a slimy trail all over the rug.

"UM OME!" wailed the creature.

"Oh, no!" said me and Tilly. The last thing we wanted to see was the Mud Creature from Planet Smelly, but there it was.

The Mud Creature had been playing soccer. Usually he had dinner at his friend Matt's house on Wednesdays, but obviously something had gone wrong.

"UM OME!" he said again.

"What's he saying?" asked Dad.

"He says 'I'm home,'" said Mom. Then she

shouted into the hallway, "Don't come in the kitchen like that!"

"Like what?" said the Creature.

"Like THAT!" snapped Mom. "You'll have to get undressed in the hall."

By now you've probably guessed that the Mud Creature from Planet Smelly was actually my big brother, James. This was not good news for me and Tilly. We started shoveling the pasta inside us as fast as we could, because we knew what was coming next.

"Did you get dinner at Matt's?" asked Dad.

"No," said the Creature. "He wasn't playing today."

Dad went to the cabinet to get another plate out.

Shovel, shovel, shovel, went me and Tilly.

"Wait, you two," said Dad. "We'll need to save a bit for James."

And sure enough, Dad spooned HUGE scoops

off both of our plates and plunked them on a plate for the Mud Creature. UNFAIR. I just hope James got all my 13 grams of fat in his portion. It would serve him right.

After we had eaten our SMALL HELPINGS of box dinner, Dad stood up and tried to look important.

"I'll leave you to clean up. I've got some work to do in my office."

Office? That sounds grand, doesn't it? I bet you're thinking that Dad's office has a big desk with lots of telephones and a giant window with helicopters outside.

Actually, it's not quite like that—surprise surprise, gosh, faint in shock.

There's a cabinet in the corner of our living

room, and one of the shelves has the computer on it. You have to get a kitchen chair and sit with your knees in the bottom of the cabinet and your bottom sticking out blocking the TV. That's Dad's office! No big desk and no helicopters. Aw, shame! Let's all weep for Dad, boo hoo hoo.

While Dad turned his computer on, Mom went to clean up the hallway. James fetched his soccer clothes and plunked them by the washing machine, but when he thought Mom wasn't looking, he dumped a huge muddy rag in the trash. I couldn't resist taking a look and giving it a poke.

"What's that?" I asked.

"Shhh!" James grinned. "It's Martha's soccer jersey."

"It's ripped to pieces!" I said.

"I know. She didn't want her mom to see it."

I wasn't surprised.

Martha lives next door at number 3, and she's awesome because she's big and jolly. Martha's mom is like an even bigger and jollier version of Martha, except for sometimes when she isn't jolly, and that's usually when Martha has been playing soccer. Martha likes a bit of pushing and shoving, so when the boys try to tackle her, it all gets pretty lively. I've seen her knock three boys over at once and then drag them along the ground while they cling to her shirt. WAHOO! GO, MARTHA!

It was a nice little bit of excitement to have Martha's old jersey secretly hiding in our trash, but another even MORE exciting bit of excitement happened next.

Dad stuck his head in the doorway. "James, you've got an email," he said.

"Me?" said James. "Who from?"

"Ho ho!" said Dad. "It's a secret admirer."

WHAT?

WOOO-HOOO!

Whizz . . . rush . . . zoom!

About half a second later, all five of us were jammed around the computer.

This is what the message said:

Dear James,

How do you do? I am your cousin Bella. Granny and Granddad say that you are the same age as me, so I am just writing to say hello. I like theater and dancing. What are your hobbies?

Please email me back.

Love from Bella

James made a face. "Who IS this?" he said.

"Your cousin," said Dad. "She's your Auntie Zoe's girl."

Oh, wow! Auntie Zoe is the coolest person in our family. I've never actually met her,* but I can tell you exactly what she looks like. She's really tall and slim with big eyes and short black hair. How do I know? Because she models dresses in the *Duchess Catalogue* that Mom reads!

(*Actually, Dad says I did meet Auntie Zoe once. I was very small and sitting on her knee, and she was wearing a light blue skirt, and my diaper was leaking a bit—EEEK! So we'll ignore that one and just say that I've never met her. The point is that Auntie Z. is a model and I'm going to be a model too, so we're soul mates. Yahoo, awesome!)

Dad stood up and made us all shuffle around so that James could sit down at the computer.

"What am I supposed to do?" moaned James.

"You'll send her a nice reply," said Mom. "We never see Zoe's family these days. It's very kind of Bella to get in touch."

"But she put 'Love from Bella' at the end," moaned James. "I won't have anything to do with that!"

"She was just being friendly," said Dad. "Now get on with it."

We all stood around James waiting for him to type something, but all he did was blush bright red. Ha ha, love it!

"Do you MIND?" snapped James. "This is private!"

So we all had to move away and leave him to it,

which was a little boring. Never mind. The fact was that James had gotten LOVE from a MYSTERY GIRL, so I had to rush out and tell all my friends.

It's one of those things that sisters have to do.

The Best of Enemies

I opened our front door and EEEK, there was Martha standing there about to whack me on the nose!

Actually, she wasn't. She was just reaching out to ring the doorbell, but you know what it's like when you open the door and somebody's already there. (Martha's the one I told you about who lives next door at number 3.)

"Hey, Martha," I said. I couldn't wait to tell her about James getting some LOVE from somebody. "You'll never guess what's happened!"

"Mom won't let me play soccer anymore," said Martha.

"No, that's not it," I said.

"Yes, it IS it!" said Martha.

Then I realized she wasn't joking. She looked really fed up.

"Is it because of your jersey?" I asked.

Martha nodded. "Partly that. But mainly what SHE said."

Martha walked back out to the street and pointed at the little fence in front of her

house. Ivy was balancing on the top, practicing tightrope walking. (Ivy is the wacky one who lives at number 7.)

"I said I was sorry," said Ivy. "It just came out."

"What came out?" I asked.

Martha explained. Basically, when she got back from the soccer game, her mom had opened the door and saw that Martha was just wearing her undershirt beneath her coat. Her mom had gone nuts about the soccer jersey and gave her a BIG TALKING-TO like moms do from time to time. In the end she said that Martha could only have another soccer jersey if she got onto the school spelling team.

"The *spelling* team?" I gasped. "What does that have to do with soccer?"

"Mom said if I had to play a sport, why couldn't I play something less messy?" said Martha.

"And I just happened to be going past . . ." said Ivy.

"No, you didn't," snapped Martha. "You came out to listen to me getting scolded!"

"All I said was 'What about the spelling team?'" said Ivy, who was still walking along the fence. "Mrs. Twelvetrees is starting a spelling club, and they're going to have a school team."

"Spelling is NOT a real sport!" moaned Martha.

"Why not?" said Ivy. "It's a team, like a soccer team."

"But I'll never get on the spelling team!" said Martha.

"I was only being helpful," said Ivy. "It's not my fault you're a rotten speller."

Martha grabbed the fence with both hands and wobbled it. Ivy fell off and skinned her knee on the pavement, which made it bleed. They both looked at me crossly to see whose side I was on.

"There's only one answer," I said. "Why don't you BOTH join the spelling club?"

"BOTH?" they both said.

"Martha will have to go anyway, but Ivy got you into it. The least Ivy can do is help you get on the team."

Ivy gave her knee a lick. "Okay," she said.

Martha looked at Ivy in surprise. "Do you mean it?"

"Of course," said Ivy. "If that's what you want."

Martha reached down and helped Ivy up. "Nasty scrape on your knee," she said. "Sorry about that."

"It'll look great in the morning." Ivy giggled.

"Yeah, all blue and scabby!" Martha laughed. "Hey, look at what I did playing soccer."

So Martha showed Ivy her knee and—*DING*—they were friends again.

Then I remembered that I was going to tell them about James and the "Love from Bella" message, but they were having so much fun with their knees, I decided I'd tell them later.

Instead I went in to see what kind of progress lover-boy had been making.

Nice and Friendly
and Boring

When I got into the living room, James was at the computer, with Dad looking over his shoulder.

"Come on, James," said Dad. "You can do better than that!"

"But I don't want to write this stupid email," said James crossly.

"Why not?"

"Because I don't even know this Bella and she put LOVE at the end!"

"So?"

"So, she's a weirdo!" said James. "Why does she think she loves me? That's gross! And now Agatha's laughing at me."

"No, she isn't," said Dad, being very serious.

Yes, she was, actually. I was trying to keep a straight face, but I couldn't help it, and neither could Dad. In fact he was trying so hard not to laugh, his nose suddenly did a big squeaky squirt.

HA HA HA HA HA!

James ran out of the room and slammed the door.

"Poor James." Dad giggled. "But we can't send this. Your mom will get mad. Look."

So I looked.

hey bella, h8 theter and h8

dansin. hobis = sokker i like the

ROVERS 4 eva. J

(If you can't understand it, don't worry. It took me a few tries, and in the end it wasn't worth it.)

Dad was right. Mom would be mad if that message got sent. What was worse is that maybe Auntie Zoe would be mad too, and I didn't want that. When I finish school and start to be a model, I might need Auntie Zoe to give me a few tips, like what expression to use when I'm having my photo taken. But what if James's message made Auntie Zoe mad at us? It could ruin all my plans for future greatness. EEEK!

"Why don't I write a message?" I said. "I'll

pretend it's from James and make it nice and friendly."

"But what if Bella writes back?" said Dad.

"Don't worry," I said. "She won't!"

It always takes me forever to type on a computer, because I like inventing little sideways faces. Here's somebody trying to lick their nose: (:-9). Ha ha! But I did this message really carefully with CAPITAL LETTERS and everything. Here's how it started:

Dear Bella,

Thank you for your message. I am a very boring person. I do not like any of the things you like. And my only hobby is

What was the most boring thing I could think of? And then I remembered Ivy and Martha fighting, and thought of the PERFECT thing! After that, the only problem was dealing with the "Love from" bit. Hmm . . . James was right. It's a bit much to be LOVING somebody you don't actually know. But it must be all right to LIKE them. That seemed fair enough. Here's how the whole message looked:

Dear Bella,

Thank you for your message. I am a very boring person. I do not like any of the things you like. And my only hobby is spelling. I think spelling is really fun. So you won't want to send me any more emails.

Like from James

P.S. Tell Auntie Zoe that Agatha is very pretty and is going to be a model too. {;-)

I'd just finished typing it out when Dad came in and looked over my shoulder.

"Clever!" he said. "But we'd better send it before James sees it."

So he clicked SEND and that was the end of that.

(Actually, you must have realized that this book has lots more pages, so of course that wasn't the end of that.)

Welcome to the Club

The next thing to sort out was getting Martha and Ivy onto this spelling team thing. We'd all been given letters to bring home about it, and mine was still in the bottom of my school bag.

I went to the hall, got my bag off the peg, and opened it up. Yuck! It's pretty gross inside my school bag, so I just shut my eyes, stuck my hand in, and hoped for the best. Here are some of the lovely prizes I pulled out:

One leaky pen with hair stuck to it.

One old cookie wrapper with hair stuck to it.

One hair bobble all knotted up with hair stuck to it.

One comb covered in jam from a random sandwich with hair stuck to it.

And finally—*TA-DA!*—

One crumpled-up letter smeared in chocolate with hair stuck to it.

I put all the other stuff back (because that's where it lives) and opened up the letter.

The new spelling club will meet at lunchtime. There will be three tests, and the best four pupils will be selected

for the Odd Street School Spelling Team! The team will compete with other schools to win books for the library.

My, my, how fun.

At the bottom of the letter was a permission slip, which you had to tear off and fill in if you wanted to join the club.

The next morning, we were all outside of school waiting for Motley the custodian to open the doors. I made sure that Martha and Ivy had their slips filled in. Ellie and Bianca came over to see what was going on, so I asked if they wanted to try out too.

"Ooh, not me," said Ellie. "Spelling tests are really scary!"

"What's there to be scared of?" I asked.

"I had a bad dream about a spelling test once. I had to spell all these different words, but I was only allowed to use the letter *g*."

Poor Ellie. Everything scares her, but Bianca's a lot braver. Maybe she'd try out?

"I better not," said Bianca. "I'm not very good at welling spurds."

"*Welling spurds?*" we all said. We love Bianca. Don't always understand her, but love her.

"Oh, I get it!" said Ellie. "She means SPELLing WORDs!"

"That's right," said Bianca. "I get the metters all lixed up."

By this time Ivy was running around the playground with her permission slip hanging out of her mouth like a long tongue. She ended up running into Gwendoline Tutt and Olivia Livid. Gwendoline lives in a really fancy house at the far end of Odd Street, and Olivia is her evil slave who probably lives in a cave somewhere and chews on bones. They're both really unpopular, so it's no wonder that nobody likes them.

Typically, Olivia snatched Ivy's slip out of her mouth and read it.

"What is this?" demanded Gwendoline.

"Ivy's joining the spelling club!" Olivia laughed.

"*Spelling club?*" repeated Gwendoline. She took the slip from Olivia and read it. "LOSERS club, is more like it! I wouldn't be caught dead doing that."

"It's going to be awesome, actually," said Ivy. "Lots of people are doing it!"

"Oh, yeah?" said Gwendoline. "Who else is a big loser?"

We all looked at Martha, but Martha just kicked the ground and kept quiet. Gwendoline threw the slip back at Ivy. Then Gwendoline and Olivia wandered off laughing.

"I've changed my mind," said Martha. She got her permission slip out of her pocket and looked around for the trash can. "I don't want to do it."

"But then you'll never get to play soccer again!" I said.

"Do I have to do it if Martha doesn't?" asked Ivy.

"If Ivy doesn't, then I'm definitely not," said Martha.

Ooh, I hated Gwendoline Tutt sometimes! Well, most times, actually.

"Give me those!" I said, taking the slips from them. "I'll hand them in so you BOTH know that you're BOTH doing it."

Martha and Ivy looked a little sulky.

"But what about Gwendoline laughing at us?"

"Don't worry about Gwendoline." I promised them, "She won't be laughing for long."

I dug my hand into my bag. It's lucky I'm organized! I'd put my spelling club letter back in along with all the other stuff, and it still had a blank permission slip to tear off at the bottom. Ha ha—I knew just what to do!

At recess time, I went to hand the permission slips in to Miss Wizzit at reception. This sort of thing is never easy, because it doesn't matter who you are or what you want, Miss Wizzit always makes it obvious that she's far too busy to help. You could be Queen Cleopatra with your pants on fire, but Miss Wizzit would still make you wait until she'd finished finding the end of the tape roll, or polishing the photocopier.

Today she was in an extremely far-too-busy-for-anything mood because Miss Barking was hanging around watching her. Miss B. is the vice principal, who has big square glasses like TV screens and always carries a folder full of boring forms to fill in.

I don't know what Miss Barking wanted, but whatever it was, she wasn't getting it. Miss Wizzit was madly stapling lots of things together—*CHONK, CHONK, CHONK*. I had to wiggle the permission slips at her forever before she snatched them, banged a staple through them—*CHONK*—and chucked them in a drawer. At least it gave Miss Barking something to talk about.

"Miss Wizzit!" said Miss Barking. "Those are permission slips."

"I know," said Miss Wizzit. "But they're only for the spelling club."

"Only?" said Miss Barking. "ONLY? You need

to put all those names on the dangerous-activity register."

"Why?"

"Lunchtime . . . spelling words . . . children . . . Isn't it obvious?"

Miss Wizzit shook her head.

"What if one of the children was injured with an oversharpened pencil?" said Miss Barking. "Or swallowed a book? Or got a finger trapped inside a piece of folded paper?"

Miss Wizzit wasn't impressed. "I'm surprised I don't need a permission slip to use my stapler," she muttered.

"You mean you haven't got one?" Miss Barking gasped. "Stop at once!"

She hurried over and took Miss Wizzit's stapler from her. Then she opened up her folder and fumbled for a "Stapler Usage in the Workplace" form or something crazy like that.

Poor Miss Wizzit. She loved her stapler, but even she had to give in when Miss Barking was handing forms out.

Miss Wizzit snatched the slips back out of the drawer and flicked through them. "Ivy Malting," she said, reading aloud. "And Martha Swan. And . . . what's this?"

It was a third permission slip, but it was a bit hard to read because it was all crumpled and had a bunch of hair and chocolate stuck to it. Miss Wizzit waved it in my face.

"Wizzit?" asked Miss Wizzit.

"It's Gwendoline Tutt," I said.

"Gwendoline Tutt?" Miss Wizzit made the sort of face that you can only make if you're Miss Wizzit and you've just found out that the most spoiled girl in school wants to join the boring spelling club.

I smiled sweetly. "Gwendoline is spelling crazy. There's no stopping the girl. Honest."

And I toddled out of reception, leaving Miss Wizzit still staring at the hairy permission slip.

My work was done. *Tum-tee-tum. Diddly-dum.*

What???

That evening Dad was being strange.

He didn't say much during dinner. He just kept giving me funny looks and winking when nobody else was watching. Then, as soon as the others were out of the way, he called me into the living room and opened the cabinet door. His computer was already on, and there was an email on the screen.

Dear James,

THANK YOU FOR YOUR MESSAGE! I can't believe it! Spelling is my FAVORITE thing too!!!! I hate theater and dancing. I only said I liked them because my mom said it would make me sound more interesting. I am on the school spelling team and we practice every recess. Today I got NECESSARY, POISONOUS, and AUTOGRAPH all correct! What's your favorite word?

Love from Bella

WHAT?????????

Zogs and Debras

I know that last chapter was pretty short, but nothing else happened. Dad had no idea what to do, so we just zapped the email. Deleted it. Killed it. Trashed it. I mean, honestly, how could anyone reply to that? So, moving on . . .

It was lunchtime on the first day of spelling club. Mrs. Twelvetrees was standing in the corridor outside the library. She's our principal and wears lots of lipstick and jangly necklaces.

"Come in, come in, one and all!" she was calling out. "Don't be shy, gang. Give it a try!"

Me and Ivy and Martha were hanging around at the end of the corridor, and we had Ellie and Bianca with us too. So far, only three people had gone in. They were Hannah, Nicola, and Andrew from James's class.

"They'll get on the team for sure," said Martha. "Those three eat books for breakfast. What chance have I got?"

"You'll be fine," I said. "The team has four people, so they need one more."

"Come on, Martha," said Ivy. "It's just a little spelling test. Let's get in there."

Ivy grabbed Martha's sleeve and tried to pull her

along, but Martha grabbed on to the radiator. Even with Bianca and Ellie pushing too, Martha wasn't going to budge.

"It's all right for you, Ivy," said Martha. "You're good at spelling."

"I promise I'll get them all wrong," said Ivy.

"But I'll get them all wrong too," said Martha. "I know I will, and then I'll look dumb."

"Don't worry, Martha," I said. "It's the first week, so it'll just be easy words."

"Like *zog* and *debra*," said Bianca.

"*Zog* and *debra*?" repeated Martha.

"She means *DOG* and *ZEBRA*!" I said. "But Bianca's right. It's bound to be animals because they're easy. And they always ask for *zebra*—it makes you practice writing a *z*."

"Maybe you'll get *cat* and *fish*," said Ellie. "Or *lion*. Or *sheep*."

"I can spell animals!" said Martha.

She smiled a big smile and let go of the radiator.

"How about *rhinoceros*?" said Ivy. "That's an animal. Or *hippopotamus*?"

"Eeek!" yelped Martha, and she grabbed the radiator again.

"You won't get anything as hard as that!" I said. "Mrs. Twelvetrees won't want to scare people off."

Martha took a deep breath and let go again.

"Okay, Ivy," she said. "Let's do it."

They were setting off down the corridor when Gwendoline came by.

"Hello, losers!" said Gwendoline. "On your way to spelling club? Or is spelling a bit too exciting for you?"

Martha ran back and grabbed the radiator AGAIN.

"Well, THANKS A LOT, Gwendoline!" snapped Ivy as Gwendoline swaggered on past us.

"Relax," I said. "Watch this, Martha."

Just as Gwendoline reached the library, Mrs. Twelvetrees put on her biggest smile.

"Ah, Gwendoline!" gushed Mrs. T. "So glad you could make it."

"What? Who?" said Gwendoline. She looked around, but there was nobody else there. And definitely nobody else called Gwendoline.

"Your father is so thrilled that you're joining our little club."

"My father?" Gwendoline gasped. "What makes him think I'm doing this?"

"I told him at the school board meeting," said Mrs. T. "He's looking forward to you telling him all about it!"

What choice did Gwendoline have? In she went.

HA HA HA HA HA!

Ivy was hopping up and down with excitement.

"Come on, Martha," said Ivy. "We can do this! Let's get in there and show Gwendoline how rotten she really is!"

A big smile crept across Martha's face. "*Dog* and *zebra*?" she asked me.

"*Dog* and *zebra*," I assured her.

"Let's go!" said Martha.

"YAHOO!" shouted Ivy.

The two of them stuck their arms out like air-plane wings and then charged down the corridor into the library, almost knocking Mrs. Twelvetrees over.

"Golly," said Mrs. Twelvetrees.

Me and Bianca and Ellie decided to hang around and wait. We probably talked about something, but I can't remember what, so here's a poem instead:

> **Tinky tonk**
>
> **Tiddly plop**
>
> **Tick tock**
>
> **Went the clock**

(Okay, I admit it needs work, but at least it passed the time.)

The door opened again, and Mrs. Twelvetrees let everybody out.

"There," said Mrs. T. "Wasn't that thrilling? I'll see you all next time!"

Out came Hannah, Nicola, and Andrew, looking happy. Then Ivy and Martha came out NOT looking happy. Finally Gwendoline shoved her way out between them.

"Ha ha, losers," said Gwendoline. "You got them all wrong!"

"Big deal," said Ivy. "You only got one right."

"Then that beats you, doesn't it?" said Gwendoline. "And I wasn't even trying."

Off she went down the corridor, knocking into people and laughing.

"What happened?" I asked them.

"It's not like spelling words in class," moaned Ivy. "To get on the team, you have to get three special words right. Mrs. Twelvetrees calls them her 'star words' and they're the hardest!"

"You said we'd get animals like *dog* and *zebra*," moaned Martha.

"Didn't you get *zebra*?" said Bianca. "That's a shame. Zebras are whack and blight and they eat grots of lass."

"I DON'T CARE!" snapped Martha.

(Poor Bianca! I'll put her zebra facts in at the back of the book to make up for it.)

"So what words did you get?" I asked.

"*Necessary*," said Ivy.

"*Poisonous*," said Martha.

"That's unfair!" I said. "It's only the first week. I can't believe they made you spell *necessary* and *poisonous* and *autograph*."

Suddenly they were all looking at me.

"Autograph?" Martha gasped.

"How did YOU know *autograph* was the other star word?" asked Ivy.

It was a good question. How DID I know? I was pulling my hair like mad. It's what I always do to wake my brain up when I'm thinking. Then suddenly I remembered—those were the three long words that were in Bella's email. WHOOO, SPOOKY!

There was only one possible explanation.

Bella's teacher must have been using the same lists of spelling words as Mrs. T. They probably got them from some secret teacher page on the Internet. The only difference was that Bella's teacher was a week ahead. Ooooh . . . !

I must have had a big grin on my face, because Martha poked me crossly.

"What's so funny?" she demanded.

"I know how we can get you on the spelling team!"

Inside Information

That night I told Dad I felt a bit mean about deleting Bella's message. He was surprised, but he said I could send her more messages so long as I kept them nice and friendly. So, nice and friendly it was, then . . .

Dear Bella,

Thank you for telling me your words. We never get words like that. My hardest word was ZEBRA.

Tell me what words you get next time. I'm really interested. Honest I am.

Like from James

Then there was a day in between when nothing much happened (it was a bit of a "Tinky tonk, Tiddly plop" day, actually), but the next night I got this:

Dear James,

I LOVE your messages! Just today we got
FOREIGN, ADDRESSES, and SPAGHETTI.
Tell me more about yourself. I've got long brown
hair and I'm the tallest in my class. What do
you look like?

Lots of love from Bellz

YAHOO! Good for Bella. I carefully copied the
words out onto a piece of paper. It looked like this
could work!

Ivy Malting and Her Secret-Message-Sending Leg

The next day at lunchtime we were all outside sitting on the bench. Martha and Ivy looked at the bit of paper I was holding. It had *foreign, addresses,* and *spaghetti* on it.

"Are you sure those words are on the test?" asked Martha.

"It's worth a try," I said.

"Maybe not," said Martha, sounding worried. "It's not fair if I know what words are coming and the others don't."

"But it's going to be you or Gwendoline who gets the last place on that team," I said. "And Gwendoline never even wanted to do it in the first place."

"If you beat her, you'll be doing her a favor," said Ivy.

"Would I?" asked Martha.

"Oh, yes!" we all said. "Definitely."

"Well, okay, then," said Martha. "I'll give it a try."

Martha stared at the words on the paper, then shut her eyes.

"F-O-R-R-I-N," said Martha.

"That's not even close to how you spell *foreign*!" I said.

"Thank goodness for that," said Martha. "I was trying to spell *spaghetti*."

HA HA HA HA HA!

We were glad Martha could joke about it, but how was she going to spell the words right on the test?

"You could take that bit of paper in with you," said Ivy.

"Too risky," I said. "Mrs. Twelvetrees might see it."

"Then you'd tree in big bubble," said Bianca.

Bianca was right. And even though Mrs. Twelvetrees is really nice, she is the principal, so you don't want to tree in big bubble with her.

"You need to write the words down somewhere less obvious," I said.

"Martha could write them on the back of her hand," said Ivy.

"Still kind of obvious," I said.

"I suppose so," said Ivy. Then she pulled her sock down to see how the scab on her knee was doing . . . and accidentally gave me a brilliant idea!

"Hey, Martha," I said. "When you tried out, where did the two of you sit?"

"Ivy was at the desk next to me," said Martha. "But there was a gap in between so we couldn't copy."

"A gap?" I said. "That's perfect. So could you look down and see Ivy's legs?"

"Well, I could if I wanted to," said Martha with

a strange expression on her face. "But why would I want to see Ivy's legs?"

Oh, honestly! Do I have to explain EVERY-THING?

At least Ellie and Bianca had understood. Bianca got one of her thick art pens out of her bag and then passed it over to Ellie, who can write neatly without crossing anything out.

Soon Ellie had written the three words in big letters on Ivy's leg. Then Ivy pulled her sock up to cover them. When it came time for the spelling test, all Ivy would have to do was pull her sock down, and Martha could copy the words out. Perfect!

But then Gwendoline Tutt came marching over, looking smug.

"Are you two ready to lose again?" Gwendoline said. "Because I've been practicing."

"Practicing?" I said. "Why do YOU want to be on the spelling team?"

"My dad said he'll give me my own laptop if I get on," said Gwendoline. "A PINK one."

"Then tough luck," said Ivy. "Because Martha will get on the team, not you."

"Martha?" said Gwendoline with a horrible

laugh. "Are you serious? I don't even know why she's bothering."

Gwendoline set off to go to spelling club. I was really wishing I hadn't put her name on that permission slip. Never mind—she was going to be in for a surprise!

Ivy looked inside her sock to make sure the words were still there. Then she and Martha went to spelling club too. Me and Ellie and Bianca waited outside like we did before.

Tinky tonk

Tiddly plop

Tick tock

Went the clock

(It might not be very good, but you have to admit it's catchy.)

This time when the club had finished, Ivy and Martha came out with big happy faces.

"Ivy's leg worked perfectly," said Martha. "But how did you know what words it was going to be?"

"James's girlfriend told me," I said.

"I didn't know James had a girlfriend," said Martha.

"Neither does he!" I said.

They all gave me a funny look, but they knew it was better not to ask questions. The good news was that Martha had gotten the star words right! But there was also some bad news, and it was stomping down the corridor toward us.

"Well, well, well," said Gwendoline. "Imagine Martha getting them all right!"

"You got two right," said Martha, trying to be nice. "So you did very well."

"Don't give me THAT!" said Gwendoline. "You were just lucky, but next week is the last test. I'll beat you, and it'll be ME on the team."

Too Many Xs!

I love it when my plans work, so I couldn't wait to give it another try. All I had to do was send Bella a nice reply to her last message and get the star words for the final test. There was just one little problem. Bella's last message was going to be a bit harder to reply to!

If you want to check, turn back to page 64. You'll see that Bella sent *Lots of love*. Yuck! And she called herself *Bellz*. YUCKY YUCK! And she even asked what James looked like. BLURGHH! It was a good thing there was only one more spelling club meeting to go before the team was picked.

Here's the message I sent back to Bella. (And try not to laugh. I was doing it for Martha, remember?):

Dear Bella,

I'm very tall like you and I've got brown hair like you and I am very handsome with big muscles.

So what words did you get today?

Love from James

Dad was starting to wonder what was going on with all these messages.

I told him I was just keeping Bella happy, which was true. After all, she was getting lovely messages

from a very handsome James with big muscles. Ha ha, it's a good thing she didn't know the truth!

Bella sent a message back the next day, so I got a pencil and paper ready to write the words down. But this is what it said . . .

Dear James,

You put LOVE FROM JAMES on the end! I'm so happy! Have you got a girlfriend? And call me Bellz!!!

LOTS of love, Bellz xxx

EEEK! I didn't want to get into this girlfriend-boyfriend thing. I tried again . . .

Dear Bellz,

You didn't tell me your spelling words! Please do, because I think they are really interesting.

Love from James.

But here's what came back:

Dear James,

Tell me if you've got a girlfriend first.

OODLES OF LOVE from BELLZ xxx

Oh, drat! Oh, well, at least my next message didn't have any lies in it . . .

Dear Bellz,

No, I haven't got a girlfriend. I can't wait to know what words you got!

Love from James

Surely that HAD to be the last message I needed to send. I couldn't think of anything else I could put in it. I was calling her Bellz, I'd put "Love from," and I had told her James had muscles and he wasn't married or anything.

But even if I'd run out of ideas, Bella hadn't . . .

Dear James,

If you haven't got a girlfriend, then you can put an X after your messages if you like. I won't mind!

LOVE AND HUGS, BELLZ XXXXX

I gave in. (Warning: The old man who types these books out for me was nearly sick when I told him about the next bit. It's so gross that you might want to read it with your eyes shut. Good luck!)

Dear Bellz,

I love you so much even more than spelling and I really hope you can be my girlfriend because you are so lovely especially if you tell me what spelling words you got in your last test.

Lots and lots and lots of love from James

XXXXXXXXXXXX

I didn't have to wait long.

Dearest James,

I'd do anything for you . . . OBSESSED,
INFATUATED, BERSERK.

LOVE, BELLZ XXXXXXXXXXXXXXXX
XXXXXXXXXXXXXXXXXXXXXXXXXX
XXXXXXXXXXXXXXXXXXXXXXXXXX
XXXXXXXXXXXXXXXXXXXXXXXXXX
XXXXXXXXXXXX . . .

. . . and all the *XXX*s filled up about three screens
on the computer. EEEKY FREAK!

While I was copying the spelling words down,
Dad was looking over my shoulder at the screen.

"What's all that about?" he asked.

"It's Bella's way of being nice and friendly," I
said.

"Yikes!" said Dad. Then he gave a little laugh. "Your mom used to send me messages like that."

"So what do we do?" I asked.

Dad pushed the DELETE button.

The message disappeared forever.

"It's for the best," said Dad.

The Lesson

On Monday when we got to class, Miss Pingle was messing around with her computer.

"Settle yourselves down, children," she said. "I'm doing a little job for Mrs. Twelvetrees."

Ha ha! That's a joke.

Miss Pingle is a new teacher and there are lots of fabulous things about her. One of them is her hair, which changes color every week. (This week's color = lemon. Crazy!)

About the only thing she isn't fabulous at is computers. She was wearing a serious expression and wiggling the mouse. Then she got up and went over to the printer in the corner. She flipped a switch on the wall and stared at the printer hopefully. Oh, dear. The printer didn't do anything, but behind her, the whiteboard came on. As the screen slowly got brighter, we could see she had been on the Internet.

"What's on the computer?" asked Ivy. "Have you been buying something?"

"What?" said Miss P. Then she noticed some fuzzy writing was appearing on the board. "Oops! You're not supposed to see that!"

She hurried back to the computer. *Click click
twiddle!* The screen went blank, and then the
printer in the corner started buzzing.

"Yippee!" said Miss P. "I did it!"

She held her hand out and marched along the front of the class, giving everybody high-fives. YO, MISS PINGLE!

She got the piece of paper out of the printer, folded it up neatly, and put it on her desk.

Hmm . . . interesting! So Miss Pingle had printed out something for Mrs. Twelvetrees, had she? Something we weren't supposed to see? Maybe it was the words for spelling club!

"What's that?" asked Ivy.

"It's private," said Miss P.

Ha! It was *definitely* the words for spelling club.

"Now, then, everybody," said Miss Pingle. "Today we're studying India."

She pushed another button and the screen came on again, but it didn't look much like India. It looked more like a pair of long red boots on sale for $24.99.

HA HA HA HA HA!

"That's not India!" we all shouted.

Poor Miss P. started stabbing at the computer, but the boots stayed there.

"You'd look good in them," said Ivy.

"Do you think so?" said Miss Pingle.

"Are you getting them?" asked Matt.

"Thinking about it," admitted Miss P.

Just then the door opened and in came Mrs. Twelvetrees.

"Good morning, gang!" said Mrs. T.

"Good morning, Mrs. Twelvetrees," said everybody.

Mrs. T. went over to Miss P., who handed her the piece of folded paper.

"Thank you, Miss Pingle," said Mrs. T., but then she looked up and saw what was on the whiteboard.

"Miss Pingle!" she said crossly. "Why do you have those boots on the board . . . for twenty-four ninety-nine?"

"I'm sorry," said Miss P. "It was my mistake."

"No. It was MY mistake," said Mrs. Twelvetrees.

Miss Pingle looked puzzled, but then Mrs. T. burst out laughing. "Yes, I made a big mistake. I got exactly the same boots myself, and I paid seventy dollars!"

Mrs. T. headed toward the door but then turned back and waggled her piece of paper mysteriously. "Martha? Ivy? I'll see you at lunchtime, girls!"

Off she went, and then India turned up on the board and we all learned about where tea bags come from. How interesting. They also make coffee and rice and curry stuff—YUM! So let's have a round of applause for India: clap, clap, clap.

Martha's Funny Mood

At lunchtime, we were all on the playground getting Ivy's leg ready for the spelling test.

Ellie had Bianca's pen and the list of words, but Martha was in a funny mood.

"It's not going to work," said Martha.

"Why not?" I said. "Ellie's all ready to write the words, so we just need Ivy to pull her sock down . . ."

And that's when I saw the problem. Ivy was wearing blue tights. EEEK!

But there's no stopping Ivy. She started wiggling like a worm in a frying pan.

"What ARE you doing?" I asked.

"I'm pulling my tights down, of course," said Ivy. "Then Ellie can write on my leg and I'll pull them up again."

"So what happens during the test?" I asked. "Are you going to pull your tights down again?"

"Why not?" said Ivy. "Nobody will notice."

But everybody on the whole playground had noticed! They had all stopped whatever they were doing and were looking our way.

"Thanks, Ivy," said Martha. "But don't bother. I'm not going to spelling club."

"But they're choosing the spelling team today," said Ivy.

"Martha," I said, "there's a soccer game tonight. Don't you want to play?"

"Of course I do! But Gwendoline deserves to get on the team more than me."

"Why?" we all said. "She's HORRIBLE!"

"Not as horrible as me," said Martha. "She's not cheating. I am."

"But you thought it was funny last time," said Ivy.

"That's because it didn't matter," said Martha. "They weren't choosing the team then, but this time they are, and Gwendoline's been practicing her words all week."

As soon as Martha said it, I realized she was right.

"Pull your tights up, Ivy," I said. "If Gwendoline really has been working to win this, then what we're doing is wrong."

"Wrong? What's wrong?" said a voice behind us. It was Mrs. Twelvetrees . . . PANIC!

She must have come out of the side door when we weren't looking. How much had she heard? Ellie was trembling so much, she dropped the list of words on the ground.

"Don't litter," said Mrs. T. "Pick it up, Ellie, and give it to me. I'll toss it in the library trash can."

Ellie blushed bright red like a tomato. What would happen if Mrs. T. saw the words on the paper? Ellie was so frozen in fear that she couldn't move.

"I'll get rid of it," I said helpfully.

But before I could grab the list, Mrs. T. stopped me.

"No!" said Mrs. T. "Ellie dropped it, so Ellie can pick it up."

She stood there holding her hand out, waiting for Ellie to give her the paper. It was awful. None of us knew what to do, and then Ellie started to cry.

"Oh, golly," said Mrs. Twelvetrees. She sounded sorry. "Don't get upset, Ellie! One little piece of dropped paper isn't going to make the school fall down."

Mrs. Twelvetrees suddenly bent over and picked the paper up herself. Then she stood there, twisting it in her fingers.

"Cheer up, girls!" she said brightly. "We've got spelling club in five minutes."

She waved the paper in our faces.

"And you'll never guess what the star words are!" she said.

Then, without thinking, she shoved the paper in her pocket and went back inside.

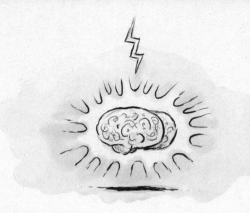

Ellie Makes Me Jealous

That afternoon was NOT a lot of fun.

Martha and Ivy hadn't gone to spelling club. What was the point? Martha was never going to get on the spelling team. Even worse, what would happen if Mrs. Twelvetrees found our list of star words in her pocket? Martha would be in such trouble that her mom would never, ever let her play soccer again EVER.

No wonder Martha spent the whole afternoon with her arms wrapped around her head.

It was almost as bad for Ellie. She sat next to Martha and kept whispering "Sorry" to her and trying not to cry. Poor Ellie. All she'd done was drop a piece of paper, but it had ruined everything.

The worst thing for me was that it was all my fault, because I was the one who'd told Martha to cheat—and I shouldn't have done that, even if Gwendoline Tutt is totally evil. I HAD to do something about that piece of paper in Mrs. T.'s pocket, but what?

Finally we heard Motley ring the bell for the end of school.

"Pack up your things, children," said Miss Pingle. "Leave your desks tidy!"

The boys all jumped up and charged out of the door like boys do. Martha got to her feet, wiped her nose on her sleeve, and picked up her bag.

"Sorry, Martha," said Ellie. "Sorry. Sorry. Sorry, sorry."

Martha completely ignored her and didn't wait for any of us. She just pushed her way out of the classroom, so Ivy and Bianca chased after her to see if there was anything they could do. I was going to go with them, but Ellie caught my sleeve. She had big red eyes where she'd been rubbing them.

"Agatha," she said, "will you stay after with me?"

"What's up?"

"I need to talk to Miss Pingle."

Wow. Ellie is scared silly about talking to teachers. What was she going to say? Soon there were just the three of us in the classroom.

"Are you all right, Ellie?" asked Miss Pingle.

"Martha's upset," said Ellie. "It's all my fault."

"Your fault?" asked Miss P. "Why?"

"I copied some words off the board that I shouldn't have," said Ellie.

"What words?" said Miss P.

"When you printed out the spelling words for

Mrs. Twelvetrees, it came up on the board, and I didn't know what it was, so I just thought we had to write it down."

What *was* Ellie talking about? I hadn't seen any words. It had been too fuzzy! But did Miss Pingle know that?

"Oh, no!" said Miss P. "That was my silly fault. I turned the screen on by accident."

"And I wrote it down," said Ellie.

Suddenly I understood.

Goodness me, Ellie Slippin! I thought to myself. *That is GENIUS!*

Ellie had just come up with a perfect explanation of how she came to be holding a list of the spelling words. If Mrs. T. found it, nobody would

be in trouble. YO, ELLIE! GOOD ONE! I so wished I'd thought of that. Cross, cross, jealous, jealous.

"So why is Martha upset?" asked Miss Pingle.

But Ellie was biting her lip and staring at the floor. She'd obviously been practicing the first part in her head, but that was as far as she'd gotten. Never mind. I could take it from there!

"Ellie showed us her piece of paper," I said. "But when Martha realized it was the spelling words, she couldn't take the test. Otherwise it would have been cheating."

"That was very honest of her!" said Miss P.

"Yes, but now her mom's going to be mad at her."

"Why?"

"Because she's desperate for Martha to get on the spelling team. It could be nasty. She'll be waiting for Martha at the school gates right now."

"Will she?" said Miss P. as she was already hurrying toward the door.

"Big lady in a red coat," I called out as Miss P. shot off down the hall.

WAHOO! Ten out of ten and a gold sticker to Miss Pingle. She is going to get a big box of chocolates from me at the end of the year. And I mean SERIOUSLY big.

Miss Pingle to the Rescue

After school, the boys were going crazy on the playground. They were warming up for the game by charging around with a soccer ball and being a **complete pain.** The worst one was Danny Frost, who always runs with his head down, and charges into everybody and everything—WHAM BASH DONK. We call him the Boy with the

Ten-Ton Head. It's amazing that the school has any walls left after Danny's been playing, ha ha!

The usual bunch of moms was hanging around by the gate, including Martha's mom in her big red coat. Ellie Slippin's mom was letting her hold Ellie's baby sister, Bubbles. Martha's mom was asking Bubbles deep questions such as "Who's a boot-i-ful likkoo girl, then?" when Martha came out the school door.

Usually Martha would toss her bag down by the railing and get into the game with the boys, but this time she didn't bother. Even when the ball rolled toward her, she didn't kick it back. She just walked past her mom, headed out the gate, and set off up Odd Street.

Martha's mom couldn't go because she was still

holding the baby, and that's when Miss Pingle came hurrying out the door.

"Mrs. Swan?" said Miss Pingle. "I'm glad I caught you!"

"Oh, dear," said Martha's mom. "Nothing serious, I hope?"

"Oh, no!" said Miss P. "I just wanted to say how sorry we are that Martha isn't on the spelling team."

"Isn't she?" asked Martha's mom.

"But she tried so hard!" said Miss P. "It's my fault she didn't make it."

"Your fault?"

"Oh, yes," said Miss Pingle. "I accidentally showed her the list of words before the test, so Martha refused to take part. She said it would be unfair to the others."

"Did she?" said Martha's mom. "Did she really?"

"I know she's terribly disappointed," said Miss P. "But it was a very honest thing to do. You must be very proud of her."

Martha's mom looked up the street to where

Martha was leaning against their front gate, looking as sad as a wet cat.

"You say she's been trying hard?" asked Martha's mom.

"And she's been very honest," said Miss P.

Guess what happened next?

I'll give you a clue. Martha's mom passed Bubbles back. Then she quickly borrowed some money from Ellie's mom and ran off to the sports supply store.

I toddled home and waited, because I knew that in about ten minutes' time there was going to be a loud knocking on the door and Martha would be standing there showing off her new soccer jersey.

It was obvious, because Martha's mom is really nice. All she had needed was the smallest excuse to let Martha play soccer again. So let's have a round of applause for Martha's big jolly mom: clap, clap, clap.

So there I was waiting at home . . . and sure enough about ten minutes later there was a knock on the door. Ha ha, good old Martha! I went to the hall and took a deep breath. I knew Martha was going to give me a monster hug, so I thought I'd better be ready. Yahoo, here we go!

I opened the door.

"I'm Bella," said a girl. "Where's James?"

Who?

I slammed the door shut.

I was having the WEIRDEST daydream. Somehow I'd gotten this picture in my head of a girl outside our front door. She wasn't much bigger than Tilly and had curly blond hair. She'd turned up with oodles of love and hugs, looking for James, and it wasn't the normal James, either! She was expecting a tall, handsome version of James, complete with muscles, who would talk about spelling and would then go on to give her three computer screens' worth of kisses. EEEKY FREAK!

I took a deep breath, then let it out slowly.

Phew!

That felt better. I even started to laugh. Honestly, James with muscles? And spelling? And *kissing?* HA HA HA . . . *argh!*

There was another knock on the door.

Very carefully I opened it, and this time I found myself face-to-face with a tummy.

It was a very slim tummy in a cream sweater. Looking down, I saw a short black skirt, long suntanned legs, and shiny red high heels. Looking back up past the tummy, I saw a chunky necklace. Then high up on top was a face with big dark eyes and short black hair.

"You must be Agatha," said the tall lady, and

then she smiled, and her mouth went right from one ear to the other and she had about two hundred teeth. "You won't remember me. I'm your mom's sister."

"Auntie Zoe!" I gasped.

She was standing on our doorstep at number 5 Odd Street just like she was posing for the *Duchess Catalogue*. It was awesome! What was even more awesome was the car parked on the street behind her. I knew it had to be Auntie Zoe's, because it was exactly the same color as her shoes! Matching shoes and cars is the sort of thing us models do.

I heard the clumping noise of footsteps in the hallway behind me.

"Good grief!" Dad gasped. He put his hand up

and stroked it across the top of his bald head a few times. I wasn't sure why.

"Hello there!" said Auntie Z.

"Yes, gosh, hello and hello, gosh, hello, yes," said Dad. He stroked his hand across his head again. Then Mom appeared behind him.

"Zoe!" she blurted out, and immediately pushed past Dad and me and gave Auntie Zoe a big rough hug that nearly pulled her out of her shoes. "What brings you here?"

"Filming down on Main Street," said Zoe.

"Oh, WOW!" I said. "Are you an actress?"

"Hardly!" said Auntie Z. "I just sat in the back of a bank pretending to be a secretary for a commercial."

"You look fabulous!" Mom giggled.

"I'm glad you think so," said Auntie Z. "It took me three hours to get like this. And if I can borrow your bathroom, it'll take me two minutes to look like a scarecrow again."

"Come in, come in!" said Mom.

"I hope you don't mind, but we didn't know we were coming this way until today."

"We?" I said. "Is there somebody else?"

"Of course," said Auntie Zoe. "I've brought Bella to meet you."

Auntie Zoe stepped past me, and standing behind her was the girl with blond curls. Although she was small, when I got a better look at her, I realized she was at least as old as me. "Who are you?" she demanded suspiciously.

"Agatha."

"But you're supposed to be pretty," she said.

Well, honestly. Of all the nerve!

This is the girl who told James that she had

brown hair and was the tallest in her class! You just can't trust some people.

Then I remembered my really nasty thought. James was supposed to be tall and handsome, with muscles! What was she going to say when she saw him?

I didn't have to wait long to find out, because James came down the street bouncing a soccer ball. He just pushed past Bella and me and went in.

"Is that James?" She gasped.

Well, there was no point lying, was there?

"Yes," I said.

"Oh, no!" she said, looking horrified.

"What's the matter with you?" I asked.

"He's . . . he's . . . *gorgeous!*"

"James? Gorgeous?" I said.

"He's so tall. And handsome. And has muscles!" said Bella. "What's he going to think of me?"

She looked really upset. I found myself feeling a bit sorry for her, since she was obviously completely insane.

"Don't worry," I said. "He's a little shy."

"Shy? You're kidding!" said Bella. "You should see what he puts in his emails."

"He's VERY shy about emails," I said. "It's best not to mention them."

"Oh," said Bella, sounding disappointed. "Never mind. At least we can talk about spelling."

"NO!" I shouted by accident. "I mean, no, he's even more shy about spelling."

"So what can we talk about?" asked Bella.

"It's probably best just to look at him," I said. "You can admire his handsome muscles."

"Okay," said Bella with a big happy smile.

Yes, she was clearly as crazy as a cat in a car-wash. No wonder I was beginning to like her.

Don't Talk About the Diaper

Dinner with Auntie Zoe and Bella was surprisingly cool!

We were in a little bit of a rush because James had to get to the game, so Mom sent Dad out to get some emergency food. He came back with "A Real Taste of Spain," which had juicy shrimp, rice, peas, and an exciting blend of herbs. Each serving also had 322 calories, 11 grams of fat, and 1,240 mgs of sodium (no, I still don't know what that is).

But the best thing is that Dad got TWO boxes. That was enough for eight people, but there were only seven of us, so we each got an extra blob of fat and a few more mgs of sodium. YUM!

Auntie Zoe and Mom did all the talking. Tilly stared at Bella, who stared at James, who stared at Dad . . . and Dad kept staring at Auntie Zoe and stroking the top of his head.

Eventually I had to ask.

"Dad, why do you keep stroking your head?"

"I don't," said Dad, stroking his head.

"Yes, you do." Mom laughed. "You're combing your hair to look nice for Zoe."

"But I haven't got a comb!" said Dad.

"You haven't got any hair," said Tilly, which was a little unkind.

But it was still funny.

HA HA HA HA HA!

"Last time we saw Zoe, he had some hair," said Mom. "And now that we're seeing her again, Dad's forgotten that it's all gone."

"He had lovely hair," said Auntie Zoe. "Long and shiny with beautiful curls."

HA HA HA HA HA!

For some reason Dad *with* hair is even funnier than Dad without hair.

"I remember he was taking my photograph," said Auntie Zoe. "Agatha was a baby on my knee, and I was wearing a light blue skirt, and her diaper came undone . . ."

WHAT? Now, that is NOT funny. Grrr.

AGATHA and AUNTIE ZOE

"LOOK AT THE TIME!" I said, a bit too loudly, and I immediately started putting all the plates in the sink. "We have to get to James's soccer game."

"Oh, dear," said Mom to Auntie Zoe. "You've only just arrived."

"Maybe we could come along and watch too?" said Auntie Zoe.

So that's what they did.

The Surprise
Substitute

It was cold, it was muddy, and after a WHOLE
HOUR of kicking and shouting, it was still zero–
zero.

YAWN! But that's soccer for you.

Motley had set the goals up after school, and
then he'd spent the game running around the field
trying to keep out of the way. It took me forever to
realize he was supposed to be the referee, but he'd

given up on blowing his whistle, because nobody did what he said. Poor old Motley!

At least Martha was getting to play with James on the blue team. She'd turned up with her mom before the game, and when she'd shown off her new soccer jersey, everybody had cheered.

"And DON'T get it dirty," Martha's mom had shouted.

But everybody knows that a muddy Martha is a happy Martha. Sure enough, about four and a half seconds later, a boy on the yellow team had deliberately run into her and they'd both fallen over. He rolled about on the ground moaning and clutching his leg, while Martha got right back up with a big smile, all ready to take on the next one. WAHOO, GO, MARTHA! We love Martha.

Dad had joined a bunch of noisy blue-team dads who were all pointing and shouting at the game. Mom and Auntie Zoe weren't even pretending to watch. They were still yakking away like crazy. Tilly was stomping around in her rubber booties, looking for worms to squash, which left just me standing with Bella. She'd spent the whole time watching James and waving little waves at him whenever he came close.

I should have guessed what was coming.

EZ·TIRES

"James hasn't waved back once," she said. "And he didn't talk to me at dinner."

"Really?" I said, trying to sound surprised.

"Do you think James likes me?" Bella asked.

"Oh, yes, I'm sure he does," I said.

"Do you think he likes me a lot?"

"It's always hard to tell with James," I said. "He doesn't show his feelings much. He's the quiet type."

And then suddenly . . .

"GOAL!" shouted everybody.

Although I hadn't been watching, it wasn't hard to guess who'd scored.

James was jumping up and down, cheering. Then he stood there with his arms outstretched while all the others came to give him a big BOY HUG. He ran around giving them all high-fives, and finally he charged in front of us, beating his chest with his fists and shouting, "NUM-BER ONE! NUM-BER ONE!"

"The quiet type?" Bella moaned.

"He's not the quiet type! Why didn't he do that when he saw me?"

"Ah, well . . . he does like soccer," I said.

"He obviously likes it more than he likes me," said Bella sadly. "He's got a heart of mud."

She got quiet again. Oh, dear. She might have been insane, but I was starting to feel rotten about the emails I'd sent.

(By the way, you just went past the title of the book. Did you notice it? If you did, then you get a gold star and a little cheer: WAHOO!)

When the game started again, the yellow dads did some extra-loud shouting, and the yellow team woke up a bit. At one point, there was a yellow player waiting quite near the blues' goal when the ball came flying over to him. Martha was too far away to do anything, but Danny Frost was close. He put his big head down and charged.

"WAAAAAH!" shouted Danny.

His head hit the yellow boy in the tummy and knocked him over.

"Ha ha ha!" laughed all the blues.

"PENALTY!" shouted all the yellow dads at Motley.

"Is it?" said Motley. "Hang on, in that case."

Motley had put his whistle in his pocket to keep it warm, but by the time he'd got it out, a yellow had already taken the penalty kick and the score was 1–1.

Now BOTH teams had woken up, and things were getting rougher.

Two big yellows were on the attack, but Martha ran into one of them and sent him flying. That just left the other yellow to face Danny, so Danny did what Danny does.

"WAAAAAH!" shouted the Boy with the Ten-Ton Head.

But this time the yellow knew what to expect. As Danny came charging toward him, the yellow stepped aside. Danny missed and shot off the field and went headfirst into a tree. *THUNK!*

Danny sat on the ground, looking very dizzy. There was no way he could play anymore, so the blues looked around for a substitute to take his place. All the spare players had gotten so bored at the start of the game that they'd gone home, so James ended up looking at me, but NO WAY! Then he saw Bella waving her little wave at him.

"What do you want?" demanded James.

"Just saying hello," said Bella.

"Yeah, whatever," said James. "We need some-body who can play."

"Okay!" she shouted, and ran onto the field.

There was an argument about it, but Bella wasn't backing down.

"I go jogging with Mom," said Bella. "So I bet I can run faster than any of you."

The blues all turned to stare at Auntie Zoe, who looked like she could run one hundred miles per hour.

"It would help me," said Martha. "Even if she just fills the gap where Danny was."

So Bella borrowed Danny's jersey and pulled it on over her top. "You stay at the back with Martha," said James. "If the ball comes near you, don't try anything clever. Just try to kick it to one of us."

When the yellows saw great big Martha walking back into position with the little person running alongside her, they all burst out laughing.

"Ignore them," said Martha. "They're only boys."

Motley blew his whistle, and the game started again.

Tinky tonk

Tiddly plop

Tick tock

Went the clock . . .

But then suddenly something exciting happened! The ball landed by Martha. Two yellows came charging over, so Martha ran off, keeping the ball close to her feet. The yellows chased after her, but when they realized she was too big and too quick for them, they threw themselves forward and grabbed onto her jersey. Martha kept going and pulled them both along. Her shirt was stretching and stretching . . . and then a loud voice drowned out everything else on the field—

"HEY, YOU TWO!" screamed Martha's mom. "GET YOUR HANDS OFF THAT NEW SHIRT!"

But they didn't let go, and Martha didn't stop running. Martha's mom put two fingers in her mouth and made a huge loud whistle noise. Everybody stopped and looked at Martha's mom.

"IF YOU TWO DON'T LET GO, I'M BENCHING YOU!" she shouted.

Motley came running over.

"Did you whistle?" he demanded. "You're not allowed to whistle. I'm in charge."

"Oh, are you?" said Martha's mom. "Then, if that jersey gets ripped, you'll be the one mending it!"

"I warn you, madam!" said Motley. "Any more talk like that and I'll pack the goals away."

Now everyone was staring at Motley and starting to laugh. In the meantime, the ball had rolled

away and was sitting on its own in the middle of the field. I ran down the sideline to get close to where Bella was standing.

"The referee hasn't blown his whistle," I told her. "So the game's still going!"

Bella ran off like a bullet—*WHIZZ!*

She'd gotten the ball halfway to the goal before the yellows realized what was happening. Everyone suddenly charged after her, but she was miles ahead.

"Pass it!" shouted James, trying to catch up. "Pass it to me!"

Bella completely ignored him.

There was only the yellow goalkeeper in front of her. He saw her coming and came out to dive on the ball, but Bella was moving so fast that he missed. She just ran straight into the goal with the ball rolling along in front of her.

WAHOO, GO, BELLA!

BIG HUGS AND HIGH-FIVES!

The Ending

It was late by the time we got home, so Auntie Zoe and Bella had to get going quickly.

We were all standing out by the car. Bella was ready to go, but Auntie Zoe is an auntie. The rules for aunties state that you can't leave until you've given everybody a big hug.

First she hugged James, which was funny because he got a lipsticky mark on his cheek. Even if your auntie is Auntie Zoe, a lipsticky mark from your auntie is NOT COOL—ha ha, love it, love it!

All the time she was hugging James, Dad was stroking his head so he was all ready for his big hug. Ha ha! Nice try, Dad. He did get a very big hug but NO lipstick. Aw, poor Dad! Boo hoo hoo.

Normally Tilly runs and hides from things like auntie hugs, but for Auntie Zoe she'd climbed onto the fence, so she was all ready for it.

I got the best hug, because Auntie Zoe whispered to me that she was doing a fitness DVD and maybe maybe MAYBE I could be in it! Wahoo, I might be famous. Pass the champagne, darling— *slurp, burp,* WHEEEEE!

And then Auntie Zoe gave Mom a hug, and they both started crying.

But all this hugging wasn't the most exciting thing happening on Odd Street that night! Just as they were driving off, I saw Bella give James a shy little wave through the car window . . . and James gave a little wave back! Crazy times.

So we all went inside, and Mom took me and

Tilly upstairs to get sorted out for bedtime and school tomorrow and putting socks and pants in the wash and all that stuff. I was just coming down to get a glass of water when I heard James's voice in the living room talking to Dad.

"You know Cousin Bella?" said James. "I just remembered, she sent me an email. Do you think it's too late to send a reply?"

It was WAY too late, James!

"Er . . . that depends," said Dad. "What did you want to say?"

"Nothing much," said James. "Just being nice and friendly."

Now, this is VERY private. I don't want you laughing at James. He might be a boy and horrible and all that, but sometimes he does things right.

You can only read this if you promise not to laugh or tell anybody.

Promise?

Okay, here it is:

Hi, Bella,

Thanks for being on our team. It was a really good goal.

Matt says that I have to ask if you'll come and play for us again. I hope so.

Good luck with stuff.

Love from James

Gosh, how exciting! I know what you're thinking.

Will James and Bella ever meet again?

Will they get married?

Will they go and live in a little cottage by the seaside?

Will he go bald?

Will they have 10000000 kids?

Will they all look like James—even the girls?

URGH!

What a horrible thought to end the story with, but don't worry! I promised Bianca I'd put her zebra facts at the back of the book, so at least that'll take your mind off it and leave you with nice thoughts, ha ha!

But right now, you have a choice. Since the story is over, you can EITHER have the normal ending like this . . .

THE END.

. . . OR if you think that's just a little boring, you can go for the mega-crazy BELLA sort of ending. It's on the next page. So are you ready?

Take a deep breath, and here we go . . .

THANK YOU my DARLING READER for reading my little story!

OODLES and DOODLES of LOVE and HUGS to YOU forever and ever and EVER.

See you soooooooon!

XXXXXXXXXXXXXXXXXXXXXXXXXXXX

XXXXXXXXXXXXXXXXXXXXXXXXXXXX

XXXXXXXXXXXXXXXXXXXXX

XXXXXXXXXXXXXXXXXXXXXXXXXXX

XXXXXXXXXXX. . . . *pause for breath* . . .

XXXXXXXXXXXXXXXXXXXXXXX

(I think all books should end like that, especially schoolbooks—ha ha, awesome!)

Bianca's Facts About Zebras

Bianca told me about a million zebra facts, so these are just a few of them, and I put in a WRONG fact for fun!

Can you guess which one I made up?

1) There are three different types of zebras, and they all live in Africa. There are mountain zebras (the smallest), grassland zebras (the mediumest), and extra-stripey zebras (the biggest).

2) Every zebra has a different pattern of stripes.

3) Zebras are black with white stripes, NOT white with black stripes.

4) You can tell a zebra's mood by its ears. (Warning! Ears backwards = bad mood.)

5) Zebras won't let anybody ride them. So if you see somebody on a zebra, then it's probably really a horse wearing pajamas.

6) Zebras sleep on their backs with their feet sticking up.

7) Baby zebras can run when they are one hour old.

8) Polar bears can make themselves look a little like zebras! That's because polar bears have black skin under their white fur. So if a polar bear borrows Dad's razor and shaves some lines of fur off—TA-DA!—it's got an instant zebra

costume! They could probably look like pandas, too, if they wanted.

So which fact is made up?

Answer: Number 6 is **completely made up** because zebras sleep standing up. By the way, number 8 could be true! If anybody says they've never seen a polar bear with stripes shaved in its fur, you can say maybe they HAVE but they thought it was a fat zebra. It's an easy mistake to make.